THE MYSTERIOUS PATH

SAUBHAGYA

ISBN 979-888530071-1

Contents

Preface

The story in this book is Horror, Suspicious and Mysterious. It is a story about the mystery of treasure and the three dangerous stages. Either, at first john could not understand anything but after some time he understood everything.

This book has numerous characters. It also encourages the reader to know about the mysterious.

NOTE:- The characters in this book are fictional and are not real.

The Adventurous Day

Once upon a time, there lived a boy named John Kins and his friends named Johny, James, and Peter. They were good friends. One day they decided to go on an adventure, on the very next day, they decided to meet at the place named the centerilla.

Now, the time was to move for an adventure. They started moving to the north because there was a Jungle and they have heard that in the North jungle there is a mystery. Now, they have started walking they walked for about 3 to 4 Kilometer and they were very near to the north Jungle and the time was noon, they put their camp and have their lunch then they took rest.

After taking a rest they started to move, the jungle was not so far. So, as they have entered after some time, they saw a lion. They were very frightened. As the lion was on the other side of the river so, they thought they should move from there as fast as they can to a safe place so that can put their camp as the sun was going to set after some time, they got a good place for their camp now they have set the camp but they were frightened too because in the jungle many dangerous animals were roaming. sometime later after discussing an idea struck them that for 2 hours one of the friends will be watching that if the animal arrives then we will tell to everyone and he will also wake up them.

Then one of the friends named Peter will watch for 2 hours then James, then after James, John will watch and at the last Johny, after some time everyone slept except Peter, he saw that a group of wolves was coming near to him he shouted and called everyone then as the John saw he as fast he can he took the torch and started showing to the wolves soon wolves ran.

Now the turn was of James but none of the animals came after 2 hours, John turns and he started watching after some time he heard a crying voice he went towards it. As he reached he saw no one. Still, he was not satisfied he thought about it a full night.

The Mysterious Day

Now, the voice he have heard last night. He wants to know about it, from Where it has come? , Whose voice it was?, and why was He/ She crying?. Many Questions were in his mind. To know the answer he was waiting for the night. Soon, the night arrived. He was ready with his things. As the voice reached him he took his torch and started moving towards the voice. He walked, Soon he became tired. Now, he was thinking to go back to his camp. But he has lost his way. He was thinking that now he could not come out of this huge jungle but he did not lose his faith. Now, in the morning he thought to move forward.

He started moving towards the mountain. as he have not taken his food to eat so he could not eat anything. So, he kept walking after walking he saw some fruits he started climbing the tree soon he reached and ate the fruits.

After eating the fruits he came down from the tree and again started moving to the mountains. the days passed after 3 days. in his way he saw a cave he thought to take a rest. After taking a rest when he got up he saw some stairs going downwards. He started walking down the stairs. He heard that crying sound which was coming from the last two nights was coming again from down. he thought that this time he will know e every answer. As he came down he saw someone he was like a boy. When he went near to him that boy became invisible. The boy became very frightened and nervous.

The boy who was crying was a ghost. Till that time the night changed to morning. The ghost became and the boy has fallen to the ground.

The Dangerous Day

After he got up he was very frightened. He ran out of the cave. He thought that their friends are good or they were in danger. He thought that he should now move down of the mountains. He was afraid because his plan was only to go for an adventure in the northern jungle. While coming he has seen someone moving. He thought to follow him. He started to follow him while following him went into a cave. He was trapped by kidnappers. They were talking about some treasure which is hidden and in a cave in the mountains there is a box in which a map is there to reach the hidden treasure but they have to lose a ghost there.

John thought to go there but he can not reach there because he was in a cage locked. After some days the kidnappers went out in search of food. John that this is time only to go out but he was thinking how could he go because the get was looked. He remembered that while going in search from the sound came he has also taken a needle he took it out and tried and tried, at last, he could open the door.

He ran towards the mountain at that time he was hungry too. He remembered that the tree from which he has eaten fruits. He went near the tree and took some fruits. He ate and became ready to move. Soon, he reached there he have also seen the ghost. At that, he took out his torch and went near to it. As he remembered that as the light of the sun reached the ghost it became invisible. So, he did the same and the ghost became invisible he quickly went

near the box and took out the map and ran out of the
cave.

Till that time the kidnappers reach there, they found that
boy have run.

Stage One - "The Haunted Graveyard"

After reading and understanding the map John decided to move on to Stage one - "THE HAUNTED GRAVEYARD" there was a saying that whoever goes there never comes back. But John Kins decided to take a risk he went inside the graveyard though he was a courageous boy but he was also sacred due to the environment present near him.

He started to move on the way through the map. In the first part of Stage One. John has to face the skull ghost. To defeat skull ghosts there was a clue that skull ghosts can be defeated by the light of the moon, But how could he bring the light of the moon as the clouds were there in the sky. So, he was afraid but he thought that if the clue is given then the moonlight he will get from the only. After some time he understood that if he will turn the map towards the skull ghosts then something will happen.

It worked in the joy he shouted, HURRAY! I cleared it, But the happiness was not for long as he walked towards the front he shows the ghost again and it was the last part too of Stage One, The ghost was a Dragula, this time the clue was the sunlight, this it was easy as the sun was going to rise but it was not so easy Dragula to defeat him he needs, The sunlight and his will power and that john were having so he defeated Draguls easily. Stage One - "THE HAUNTED GRAVEYARD" was cleared.

Stage Two - "The Land Underwater"

After completing Stage One - "THE HAUNTED GRAVEYARD", He came to another Stage Two - "THE LAND UNDERWATER. John could not understand the meaning so he kept moving forward after some time he saw the sea. He could not understand that he will move forward, So he took out the map and saw the clue it was written go under the sea but John didn't know to swim.

He thought that some way would be there to go, So he kept thinking, seeing the map again and again but he couldn't find the way. He thought that how he defeated the skull ghost by using the map. He would go in that way to "The Land Underwater".

So, he kept on his face the map and started going towards the down while going he found a caretaker or protector of that land. The clue was given do not to look into his eyes so he closed his eyes and started moving forward. he crossed the protector easily and he cleared Stage Two also.

Stage Three – "The Digger"

Now, the turn was of the last Stage and the most difficult Stage - "The Digger". In this stage, he has to face the Digger. John kept on moving suddenly the wind blows. he hides behind the tree. Out of the cave, Digger was standing. He was like humans only but in his face, the eyes, the nose, the mouth nothing was there. He became afraid.

In a few minutes, John seemed that someone kept a hand on his shoulders. When he turned and saw the Digg was standing back of him. He ran very fastly while running his torch fell to the ground but he kept running. While running he saw the map and asked for a clue but it was written no clue to defeat "The Digger".

He became more afraid. He saw that an old man was sitting out of the house with a lamp. John went near him. He said the full story. The old man put his lamp close to his face and asked does he was looking like him. John has fallen to the ground. Till that time sun have risen so the Digger went inside the cave, and the entrance of the cave was closed.

John got up and saw that Digger was not there. He thought about it and understood that Digger could not face sunlight. He took up his map and became ready. The night came as the Digger came out John showed him the map Digger have fallen on the ground for some time. Till that time John took the treasure and saw the map, he saw that to go out he have to take the locket of Digger he took it easy with the treasure he went out of the cave. At last, he went to his home after clearing all the stages.